Magical Sweets in Story Time

Fairy Tales &
Magical Adventures
Book Two

Merriweather Hope

Magical Sweets in Story Time

Copyright © 2014

All Rights reserved under International and Pan-American Copyright Conventions. By payment of required fees you have been granted the non-exclusive, non-transferable right to access and read the text of this book.

No part of this text may be reproduced, transmitted, downloaded, decompiled, reverse-engineered or stored in or introduced into any information storage and retrieval system, in any form or by any means, whether electronic or mechanical, now known, hereinafter invented, without express written permission of Story Time Books. For more information contact Story Time Books.

The publisher does not have any control over and does not assume any responsibility for author or third-party websites or their content.

This book is a work of fiction. The characters, incidents and dialogue are drawn from the author's imagination and are not to be construed as real. While reference might be made to actual historical events or existing locations, the names, characters, places and incidents are either products of the author's imagination or are used fictitiously, and any resemblance to actual persons living or dead, business establishments, events or locales is entirely coincidental.

Merriweather Hope

Table of Contents

Chapter 1 – Let's Try This Whole "Saving Magic" Thing Again 4

Chapter 2 – The Biggest Threat to Magic Ever! 12

Chapter 3 – The Truth about Magic 18

Chapter 4 – Not Everything You Read Is True… 25

Chapter 5 – Time Travel Can Be a Real Pain .. 31

Chapter 6 – What REALLY Happened to Hansel and Gretel 42

Chapter 7 – Don't Get Caught In a Web of Lies 50

Chapter 8 – The Bad Guy Gets Away… Again 60

Chapter 9 – Everyone Gets to Go Home With a Full Tummy 64

Chapter 10 – It's Never Too Late for Magical Adventures 69

Epilogue – Time is Running Out for Magic… 73

Don't miss book three in the "Fairy Tales & Magical Adventures" series! 78

Magical Sweets in Story Time

Chapter 1 – Let's Try This Whole "Saving Magic" Thing Again

Stefan slid down the side of the volcano with three golden goblins in hot pursuit. He clutched the key to their spaceship tightly in his right hand as he raced to where it was sitting in the clearing only a few yards away. Just then, he felt the earth strangely shudder beneath his feet.

"Oh no!" Stefan thought, "I have to get to the spaceship before the volcano erupts!"

Just as he came to a sudden stop in front of the shimmering door of the humongous green and gold space craft, he heard a loud, "Stefan...STEFAN!"

*****

Stefan sighed as his daydream came to an end as his big brother shouted his name.

"What do you want Chandler?" Stefan called back, "I'm in my room."

"I'm going out back to shoot some hoops before I go to my friend's house for dinner, you up for some one on one?" Chandler asked.

Merriweather Hope

"Aw, man!" Stefan said, "I'd love to, but I still haven't finished my homework and I don't want to get in trouble when Mom gets home."

"Suit yourself," Chandler called out as he stomped down the stairs.

Stefan heard the back door slam shut and he sighed. He really needed to pay more attention to his school work. He shook his head of messy blonde curls and tried to think about what he had to do.

After the adventures of the last few weeks, Stefan was finding it kind of hard to go back doing the things nine year-old boys usually do. Everything was boring after that. He really had to try harder. He had his regular homework to do and a Social Studies quiz on Thursday.

But he just could not keep his mind on his work. He was missing, Jinn, his own personal genie, too much. He had found her in a box of Magical Charms cereal and life hadn't been the same since. It was foolish of him to have sent her away. Since she left, things had become very boring. But he had to do it because she had caused so much trouble. Right now though, he was missing the fun things they used to do together.

Stefan's tummy gave a rather loud growl and he looked at his watch. His heart sank into his very empty stomach when he saw it was still another two hours until dinner.

"Right," Stefan said aloud, "No time for that now. I need to get this math homework done so I can study for the quiz".

He took a deep breath, shook out his fingers and looked at the next problem in his book. His brow crinkled as he tried to work out the answer. Math had never been his best subject at school and he was really very very hungry!

"Boy, I wish I had a pizza now," he said, as he pushed his chair back from his desk.

As he said this, he remembered the awesome pizza party Jinn had magically thrown for their whole school just a few weeks ago. He sighed. He must get Jinn out of his head. Maybe if he stretched his muscles for a bit he would be able to get some work done.

As he stood up, there was a knock at his bedroom door. At the same time something fell noisily onto his desk.

"Who on earth could that be?" Stefan wondered as he made his way to the door. He looked back over his shoulder and saw something golden on top of his Math book. It twinkled in the late afternoon sunlight that was pouring in through his window.

"Mmm," Stefan thought, "that looks just like...... Nah, couldn't be...."

"I have to stop dreaming," he told himself as he turned the knob to open his bedroom door.

He pulled the door open and his jaw dropped.

"Close your mouth, Stefan, anyone would think you've never seen a genie before," said Jinn, giggling as she skipped into the room carrying a box of pizza that smelled amazing!

"What....how....huh?" Stefan stuttered as he looked at his desk and saw that it was indeed Jinn's lamp that he had seen.

Magical Sweets in Story Time

"But….but…. I wished you away," he stammered.

"Yeah, and now I'm back," Jinn said smiling. "Didn't you miss me?"

"Of course I did!" said Stefan, throwing his arms around her neck and giving her a big hug. "But what are you doing back here?"

"Well…" Jinn began, but before she could say another word Stefan stopped her.

"Wait! Let me call Kaia. She'll never believe me if she doesn't see you herself." Stefan said.

Stefan dashed out the room to go call Kaia friend who lives next door. A few minutes later they both returned to find Jinn floating upside down in the air munching on a piece of pizza.

"See, I told you," Stefan said.

Kaia stared at Jinn for a minute before saying hello. They were both feeling a bit nervous at having her around again. Why had she come back? Hadn't she caused enough trouble the last time? How could she forget all that had happened? But then, they did enjoy the fun times they had together. For that they were really happy to see Jinn again. But they could not forget the trouble the three of them had gotten into and the adults were just beginning to forget. What would they say now, if they found out that Jinn had returned? This was what bothered Kaia and Stefan.

"So, what's going on Jinn?" Stefan asked through a mouthful of cheesy pizza, "How come you're back?"

"Well, remember I told you I was on some kind of job that I couldn't remember because I had fallen asleep while the Fairy Queen was telling me what I had to do?"

"Yeah," said Stefan, not sure what was coming next.

"It turns out that I was sent specially to you, Stefan, because you are supposed to help me save magic." Jinn said.

"But I'm just a kid," Stefan exclaimed in a bit of a panic. "How can I know how to save magic? I don't have any special powers or know any magic!"

Magical Sweets in Story Time

"Well, when you wished me back home, the Fairy Queen was very angry that I hadn't finished what I was sent to do. She told me that she was giving me one last chance to get it right. So I was to come back here and you are to help me use all the dusty old books that are in my lamp library to find out what we must do. If you don't help me save magic the Fairy Queen will forever be angry with me." Jinn told them. She was nearly in tears.

Stefan and Kaia looked at each other and then back at Jinn. They wanted to help her save Magic but they did not want anyone to get hurt like the last time.

"Come on guys, you have to help me," Jinn begged, "this time will be different. I know what we are supposed to be doing now and we have a ton of books to help us if we get stuck. I really need your help. I know I cannot do this all by myself," she finished quietly.

Stefan and Kaia had never seen Jinn looking so sad before. She was always so bubbly and full of life. Kaia looked at Stefan as if to say "what else can we do, we must help her."

Merriweather Hope

Stefan took a deep breath and grabbed his third piece of pizza, before saying, "Alright. We'll help you, but first you must tell us who or what are we saving magic from?"

Magical Sweets in Story Time

Chapter 2 – The Biggest Threat to Magic Ever!

Jinn clapped her hands together in glee and her many bangles jingled and jangled. Stefan and Kaia sat down on the floor next to Stefan's bed with the pizza between them. They waited for Jinn to begin the story as they watched her walking back and forth across the floor.

"Jinn," Kaia said, "You need to tell us everything if you want us to help you. We need to know what we are getting into, especially if there are any dangers."

Jinn stopped pacing and turned to face her friends. Her face was very serious.

"Okay, well I guess I should start at the beginning. I owe you guys that." Jinn said quietly.

She sat down in Stefan's chair, crossed her arms over the top of the backrest and placed her chin on her arms.

"What nobody knows, is that thousands of years ago humans and magical creatures all lived in the world together in peace. We all respected each other's differences and special abilities and there were hardly ever any problems."

"Wow! Way cool," Stefan burst out saying. "Imagine me having a pet dragon."

"Or a witch for a best friend," chimed in Kaia.

"So what happened?" Stefan asked. "How come most humans don't know about this anymore and why don't magical creatures still live with us? Why is it all such a big secret now?"

"Well, that's just it," said Jinn, "for hundreds, maybe thousands of years, everything was fine, but then something went horribly wrong. Or rather I should say, someone went horribly wrong."

For a while Stefan and Kaia sat super still waiting to hear more. Suddenly Stefan, blurted out, "Did a knight build up a fire breathing dragon army? Or did an evil witch start turning all the humans into slimy toads? Or was it goblin snot? Oh, I know, did the trolls try to take over the world?"

Magical Sweets in Story Time

Jinn giggled in spite of herself. "Ha! Ha! Stefan you have a really wild imagination," she said, pretending to scold him. She saw that his eyes were bright with excitement.

"So who caused the problem then?" Kaia asked.

"Brother Grimm," Jinn said.

"But, how can that be?" Kaia asked, "He wrote a whole bunch of children's story books. I have one in my room. So what does he have to do with the magic?

"That's just it!" Jinn exclaimed, jumping up so quickly from the chair that it fell over. She began to pace again.

"He was an evil man. He has been capturing magical creatures for ages now and trapping them in the story books that he writes!" She stomped her foot in anger as she made her point. This caused the bells and jewels on her clothes to tinkle.

"So what can we do about that?" Stefan said scratching his head in confusion, "I don't see how we can help you."

14

Merriweather Hope

"We have to rescue them!" Jinn shouted, "We need to set them free – that's our job! "

Both Kaia and Stefan did not know what to say. This sounded crazy. How were they to get into the pages of story books to save anyone?

Kaia looked over at Jinn and said, "why us? How come the rest of the magical creatures can't just go

out and get their friends? They have magical powers, we don't have any."

"Well, see, that's just it," said Jinn, "The only magical creatures that haven't been captured are the young ones, like me. Our magical powers are not strong enough yet, that's why I have the library of books to help us.

The Fairy Queen believes that the only way to save the magical realm from being destroyed by Brother Grimm, is if magical creatures and humans once again work together, side by side, to save the world. You see, while we magical creature that are left certainly have powers, we are too young to have any real experience of the world, which is why we need help from humans

Magical Sweets in Story Time

That's why I need your help. The Fairy Queen says it's up to us to rescue the magical creatures from the tales where they are trapped and return them to her. Once they are returned to the Fairy Queen, they can all join together to catch Brother Grimm. When this happens, we'll put back magic in its right place in the world."

"Okay," said Kaia, taking charge. "We won't let you down. Stefan and I will help you, but I think you'll have to promise us that you won't ask us to do anything that will cause trouble like the last time."

"Alright, I promise," Jinn said.

"Kaia said, "One. No more lies"

"Yeah," Stefan said, "and no doing of anything that will hurt other people."

"Okay, Okay, "Jinn said. "I promise. She was still feeling a little bit guilty about all the trouble that she had the last time.

"Stefan, I think we have to try not to make any wishes for any kind of stuff that does not have to do with the job…I think that caused a lot of trouble the last time." Kaia reminded him.

"Let me see if I got it right,' said Jinn, counting off the rules on her fingers. "No wishes outside of the job we are doing, do nothing that will hurt others, and no more lying."

"Kaia, you know what we have to do before we do anything else, don't you?" Stefan said in a serious voice.

"What?" said Kaia looking confused.

"We have to tell our parents the truth this time," Stefan said. "We have to let our parents meet her

and tell them what we are doing as we try to save magic.

Jinn and Kaia just stared at Stefan. What he said was true, but what would their parents have to say about it? This was going to be very interesting!

Chapter 3 – The Truth about Magic

The three of them sat looking at each other not knowing what to do. They all knew Stefan was right, but building up the courage to tell their parents the truth about Jinn was going to be something else.

The loud ringing of the phone was heard by them all.

Kaia said, "Stefan, you'd better answer it."

"Yeah," mumbled Stefan as he stood up and made his way to the door, "I'll be right back."

Stefan dashed down the hall and grabbed the telephone on the last ring.

"Hello" He listened for a few minutes and then said, "Okay, see you in a few minutes."

He walked back into his room feeling very afraid. His face must have given him away because as soon as Kaia saw him she asked.

"What's up, Stefan?"

"That was my mom," he replied, "she said you

and I need to get over to your house now. Your folks have invited my family over for dinner."

Kaia now also became afraid. "You mean we'll have to tell them now?" she asked in a shaking voice.

Stefan nodded.

"But we haven't had any time to talk about it or plan what we are going to say."

"But remember, Kaia, we're going to tell them the truth," Stefan said, hoping that one of them would say that it was not really going to be so.

Kaia looked even more troubled and Jinn did not say anything. Stefan was trying to be brave, but he was still feeling very nervous at what they were about to do.

"Come on let's go." He said and hurried them up. If he did not go quickly he was not sure he could do it.

When they arrived next door, the table was being set for dinner and delicious smells were coming out of Kaia's kitchen. The grown-ups

Magical Sweets in Story Time

were laughing and chatting as the children made their way down the hall to the dining room.

Suddenly a pain shot through Stefan's tummy and his palms began to sweat. "Oh please, please let this work," he prayed as he hurriedly wiped his clammy hands on his jeans. "I wish they would be cool about all this and understand how important it is," he muttered to himself as he took another deep breath.

Jinn's sharp ears heard what Stefan whispered to himself, and this gave her a wonderful idea.

"Hmm…," she said to herself, "only five minutes have gone and he is already breaking one of the rules by making a wish. Okay, Stefan, I'm your genie and remember that your wish is my command."

Just then Stefan caught Jinn looking at him in a very strange way. She was wiggling her fingers in the air and he saw a mischievous smile spread across her face. He hoped she was not up to any of her tricks now. They had reached the door to the dining room and were about to face their parents.

Merriweather Hope

"Hey kids," said Kaia's mom as they opened the door, "Oh, who is your friend?"

"Hi Mom, Dad. Hey Mr. and Mrs. Thompson," Kaia greeted the grown-ups, "This is Jinn. She is our genie."

"Hey everyone," Jinn said with a friendly wave that made all her bangles tinkle together musically.

Stefan and Kaia held their breath waiting to hear what the adults had to say.

"How lovely to meet you," Stefan's mom said.

"Would you like to join us for dinner?" Kaia's dad asked.

"Yes, please," answered Jinn, "I would love to."

Stefan and Kaia looked at each other in surprise as Jinn took her seat at the table. They could hardly believe their good luck. Nobody had even blinked at the word "genie".

"So how did the three of you come to be friends?" asked Stefan's dad, once they were all seated, each with a steaming plate of meatloaf in front of them.

While they ate the children told them how Jinn had been placed in Stefan's mom shopping cart inside a box of magical charms by the Fairy Queen. Jinn was on a very important mission to save magic and she needed their help.

Kaia and Stefan told the truth about all the things they had lied about when Jinn first came. They told them that it was really Jinn who had used her magic to make the sword appear as well as the wolf puppy, the pony, the archery set, the princess clothes and the fairy castle. They also explained how they had hurt their friends wishing for the lead in the school play and to win the soccer game. They also said they were sorry and it wouldn't happen again.

"We didn't want to lie to you," Stefan said, "but at that time we were afraid you would not understand."

Their parents just nodded and waited for them to continue.

"So now that we have to help Jinn save magic, we needed to tell you the truth, because Jinn is going to be around quite a lot until we can capture evil Brother Grimm and set free all the magical creatures he has trapped inside his story books."

At last Stefan was finished and he dared to look up from his plate. All the grown-ups were smiling. Huh? Stefan looked over at Kaia who seemed just as confused as mixed up as he was. They had been expecting a lot of shouting and maybe even some form of punishment!

"Ha! Ha!" chuckled Kaia's dad as he laid down his knife and fork on his empty plate.

"Kids today," said Stefan's mom as she wiped her mouth with a napkin.

"What a story!" exclaimed Kaia's mom, clapping her hands.

Stefan's dad chimed in, "Awesome tale, son. What a great imagination you have."

Before Stefan and Kaia could figure out that it was she who had made the grown-ups so understanding, Jinn jumped up and began to clear away the dinner dishes. Stefan and Kaia

Magical Sweets in Story Time

also got up to help and as they were coming back through the kitchen, they noticed the huge bright smile on Jinn's face.

"To know me is to love me," Jinn said as she carried out the last of the plates.

"Right kids," said Kaia's dad, "Thank you for clearing the dinner table. Off you go now to 'save magic', we're going out onto the porch for a bit."

Stefan and Kaia walked away feeling more than a little surprised and not quite believing their luck.

"Come on," said Stefan, let's go back to my place, I don't want to listen to all that boring grown-up talk."

They ran next door and as they got to Stefan's front door, they both noticed Jinn skipping up the sidewalk whistling a happy little tune. As she passed them and entered the house she gave them a wink over her shoulder.

"Mmm… she looks very pleased with herself doesn't she?" Kaia whispered to Stefan as she shut the door behind them.

Chapter 4 – Not Everything You Read Is True…

They all sat down on the floor in Stefan's room and Kaia let out a big happy sigh.

"Phew," she said wiping her hand across her forehead. "That went better than I expected."

"Yeah," Stefan agreed, "I didn't think it would be that easy!"

Jinn decided it was best to stop talking about what had just happened. She did not want Kaia and Stefan to know she had anything to do with it. She had simply granted Stefan his wish, which was what a genie was supposed to do. But she didn't want them to get into an argument about breaking the rules when she had just gotten them to agree to help her with her mission.

"So, what are we going to do about Brother Grimm?" Jinn asked.

"Yeah," said Stefan, "We need to come up with a plan."

"Sure!" Kaia agreed.

Magical Sweets in Story Time

But the three of them just sat there and looked at each other and not knowing what to do.

"Um...," said Kaia.

"Well...," said Stefan.

And then they both looked at Jinn.

"Well, don't ask me" she replied twirling her hair around her finger, "I was hoping the two of you would have a plan!"

"Jinn," Kaia shouted, "You should know! This is your problem and we don't know who we are fighting against. So how can we help? Maybe you need to go read some of your books and get some ideas."

"No!" wailed Jinn, "I don't want to spend my time stuck in the lamp *reading*." She spoke the word 'reading' like she was spitting out something gross like dragon poop! "Let's try coming up with something first. I promise I will go read the books if we can't think of anything."

"But how?" said Stefan, "we have no idea where to start."

"GRRR...," Kaia shouted as she stood up and stomped her foot. "This makes me so mad I wish the Fairy Queen had given us a clue as to what we are supposed to do!"

Kaia clapped her hand over her mouth as she knew what she had just said. At the same time, Jinn gave her a why-do-I-have-to-do-everything look and wiggled her fingers, sending out a stream of silver stars. They all followed the trail of stars out of Stefan's window and watched it go into Kaia's bedroom window next door. The next minute a big book came whizzing in through the window and fell to the floor. When they stepped forward to have a look, they saw that it was Kaia's copy of Grimm's' Fairytales, which had fallen open to the story of Hansel and Gretel.

Kaia, Jinn and Stefan stared at the book for a while until Stefan finally said, "Well, it must have fallen open there for a reason. Let's read the story, maybe there is a clue in it that will help us."

And so, they sat down and Kaia began to read the story out loud. She soon became very upset because Jinn kept butting and changing the story to something else.

Magical Sweets in Story Time

In the end, Kaia said, "Jinn! That isn't the story! Look at what is written here in the book. If you keep on butting in we might miss an important clue!"

"But Kaia," Jinn said, "That's just it. What you are reading isn't the right story. When I was told the story of Hansel and Gretel, the witch wasn't evil like in the one you are reading. Are you sure you are reading it right?"

"Jinn, I am 9 years old!" Kaia said in an annoyed tone, "I know how to read!"-

"Okay, I'm sorry," Jinn said, "It's just that I have always known the witch in this story to be the White Witch who baked magical treats and made delicious candies for all the children. She certainly didn't catch children and try to eat them! In the story I was told it was Brother Grimm who caught the children and said it was the White Witch. This is how he uses his sticky web of lies."

Suddenly Stefan, all excited, said, "Jinn! Kaia! That's it! Don't you see?"

"What, Stefan? What?" Kaia wanted to know.

Magical Sweets in Story Time

"Brother Grimm is the one causing the trouble…he has been telling lies about the magical creatures…" Stefan told them.

Jinn's face lit up. "You're so right. And so he uses his lies to keep them trapped in his fairytale world. Now I understand."

Everything began to make sense to the genie now. No wonder the Fairy Queen wanted him caught. Now she knew why her job was so important. This Brother Grimm had to be stopped and Kaia and Stefan were going to help her do it.

Chapter 5 – Time Travel Can Be a Real Pain

"Wow! What a mean man," Kaia exclaimed loudly. "We are going to have to stop him and let the world know that the witch isn't bad and that all these years she has been lied about. Once we set her free, the whole world will know how evil Brother Grimm really is."

"Exactly, now we know who we need to save and why, let's get going!"

They were all excited about their task and could hardly wait to do something.

"But what are we going to do?" Kaia asked as she fixed her clothes and looked out of the window.

"That's what I'm thinking and I can't come up with anything." Stefan ran his hands through his blonde curls, pulling at them as he spoke. "We need to get started right away. I wish…"

"No, Stefan, don't!" shouted Kaia. But he finished speaking before she could stop him.

Magical Sweets in Story Time

"I wish we were in the story now to stop that bad man and show everybody that the White Witch is innocent!"

Immediately, Jinn wiggled her fingers and sent three rockets of purple and pink stars shooting out of her fingers. Two of the rockets hit Stefan and Kaia squarely on the chest and the third went straight up into the air and landed on Jinn's shoulder.

The next instant they were all spinning through a tunnel of bright colors and where they were travelling at the speed of light with reds, greens and purples shooting past them in a blur. The spiral tunnel seemed to stretch on forever as they tossed and turned through it. The darker colors gave way to yellow and gold with a bright silver flash of the brightest light any of them had ever seen. They finally landed with a thud in a thick forest.

Jinn was the first on her feet and went to help Kaia who was clutching her tummy and had turned a bright shade of green.

"Are you alright?" Jinn asked.

Merriweather Hope

"Yeah," Kaia replied, "I just need a minute to catch my breath. I'm feeling so dizzy! What was that?"

"We went through a time travel tunnel, Jinn told her as if it was the most natural way in the world to travel.

"We have Stefan to thank for getting us here. This would not have happened if he had not made his wish to be in the story, it was the only way to get here." She sounded quite pleased with what had happened.

"Where is Stefan?" Kaia asked, looking around. The girls then saw him coming up from behind a blackberry bush picking brambles out of his hair and rubbing his bottom.

"Ouch!" he said as he came over to join the girls, "I have got to work on my landing!"

They burst out laughing.

"Oh look," said Stefan pointing to something that was behind the girls. "That must be Hansel and Gretel's house over there in that clearing."

Kaia and Jinn turned around and saw a small little cottage with a thatched roof. There were blue curtains in the windows and a thin trail of smoke coming up out of the crooked chimney.

"So what are we waiting for?" Kaia asked, "Let's go find Hansel and Gretel!"

She started to walk off towards the little house in the clearing, but suddenly Jinn cartwheeled past her and put up her hand, telling them to stop.

"I don't think that's a good idea," said Jinn, "I think we should stay hidden here until Hansel and Gretel meet the witch. I don't want Brother Grimm to know that we are here."

*****

Meanwhile, in the little cottage Hansel and Gretel were sitting at the old almost broken down kitchen table listening to their stepmother grumbling for about the thousandth time.

"I am so tired of being poor," she muttered, "I just want some nice things and pretty clothes. I don't think that's too much to ask, but with you two greedy children always around, we barely even have enough food!"

Hansel and Gretel looked at each other and their faces were sad. Their beautiful and kind mother had died not even a year ago and they really missed her. They wanted their dad to be happy, but they really wished he had chosen someone a little nicer to be their stepmother – someone who loved them.

She got jealous whenever their dad showed them any kind of love. Whenever that happened she was especially mean to them. They always had to do tons of chores and if she ever caught them playing, she would think up something particularly nasty for them to do. Her favorite job was to get them to scrub the big stone kitchen floor with their toothbrushes because that kept them busy for hours.

Suddenly, their stepmother yelled. "I've had enough! Something must be done about you two!" and she banged her hand on the table.

Hansel and Gretel were so frightened they held on tightly to each other.

Merriweather Hope

Stefan, Kaia and Jinn froze when they heard the screaming coming from the cottage. The next minute the door was flung open and they saw Hansel and Gretel being dragged into the forest by their stepmother.

As they got nearer to where the three of them were hiding, they heard the stepmother speaking.

"I don't know why I didn't think of this sooner. Life will be so much easier if the two of you are gone. I will have much more for myself and won't have to see your ugly faces every day."

Stefan, Kaia and Jinn, making sure they stayed out of sight, followed as the stepmother took Hansel and Gretel deeper and deeper into the forest.

What are those white things that Hansel keeps dropping on the ground?" Jinn asked, whispering.

"Those are the pebbles he collected earlier. Remember from the story?" Stefan answered.

Magical Sweets in Story Time

"They are going to follow the pebble trail back home," Kaia whispered back.

After what seemed like a very long time, the stepmother turned to Hansel and Gretel.

"Right now you two stay here. I'm going to fetch something I saw along the way. Wait right here until I get back. Don't follow me. Do you understand?"

With that, she went off by herself down the path they had come and disappeared around the bend. Poor Hansel and Gretel all alone in the middle of the forest.

Stefan, Kaia and Jinn watched as it grew dark and Gretel began to cry. As her body shook with sobs, they saw Hansel come up and give her a hug to comfort her.

"Don't worry Gretel," he said, "We will be home soon. I collected a whole bunch of pebbles in the garden this morning and I have been dropping them as we have been walking. All we have to do is follow the trail home in the morning. Stop crying now, everything is going to be alright."

Merriweather Hope

*****

The next morning dawned bright and sunny. Stefan, Kaia and Jinn stretched their bodies and silently stood up on the soft mossy ground where they had spent the night in the forest. As they peeked over a nearby bush, they saw Hansel waking up Gretel.]

"Come on Gretel," he said, "It's time to go home."

Hansel and Gretel walked hand in hand through the forest following the trail of pebbles. Near sunset, they finally saw the cottage they called home in the clearing. Slowly, they went up to the door and knocked. Jinn and the children stayed out of sight and waited behind the blackberry bush to see what would happen.

An angry stepmother opened the door and started shouting at the two children. There was much screaming and banging of things and the cries of the children came from inside the cottage.

Jinn, Kaia and Stefan did not hear everything but enough to let them know that the stepmother was being very unkind to them.

They heard when a man's voice shouted, "But they are my children!"

"Yes, but they cost too much," the stepmother shrieked.

"I can't believe you want me to me do this," said the man again.

"It's them or me!" The stepmother shouted. "I tell you, tomorrow morning, they must be gone or else…"

They did not hear any more, only a door slamming loudly.

The next morning bright and early, the door to the cottage opened. Out stormed the stepmother pushing Gretel in front of her with one hand, and dragging Hansel by the ear with the other. Behind them came Hansel and Gretel's father, carrying a knapsack and looking very unhappy. The four of them went deeper and much further into the woods than before.

"This time you won't find your way back home so easily," the stepmother said, looking angrily at them.

Hansel and Gretel were looking scared and sad, all at the same time.

"Hansel, where are the pebbles to leave a trail?" Gretel asked softly.

"I didn't have time to collect any Gretel," Hansel answered.

Gretel looked at Hansel with frightened eyes. "What are we going to do? We'll be lost forever.' " she whispered to him.

The tears started to pour down her cheeks.

Chapter 6 – What REALLY Happened to Hansel and Gretel

Hansel felt weak and helpless. It hurt to see his sister crying and unhappy. He would do anything to help her. But what could he, a little boy, do?

As he was thinking about this, he pushed his hands into his pockets and felt something in one of his pockets. It was a piece of the stale bread he got for dinner last night. As he held onto it tightly, it broke into small crumbs. That's when he had an idea!

"Gretel," he whispered, "Don't worry, I have a plan."

"What is it?" Gretel asked.

"I found a piece of bread in my pocket. I am going to use it to mark the trail just as I did with the pebbles. We'll find our way back home, so stop crying now, we are going alright. I promise." He squeezed her hand to comfort her

Gretel smiled at him through her tears and then bravely wiped the back of her hand across her eyes to dry them.

Merriweather Hope

"Thanks Hansel," she said, "I knew I could count on you, my big brother."

Stefan, Kaia and Jinn followed the four of them for what seemed like forever and just when Kaia thought there was no way she could walk another step, she bumped into the back of Stefan who had suddenly stopped walking.

"Why are you stopping, Stefan?"

"Because they've stopped, silly." And he pointed to Hansel, Gretel and their parents.

"Thank goodness!" Jinn exclaimed, "I'm tired!"

They watched as the father gave the children some food and water and hugged and kissed each one. The stepmother stood by saying nothing. They then turned and left them in the forest. The father waved until he was out of sight. Hansel and Gretel were left all alone in the forest once more. And their wicked stepmother was happy.

*****

Hansel and Gretel looked around.

Magical Sweets in Story Time

"Let's wait until they are gone a while before we follow the trail of bread crumbs." Hansel told his sister.

So they rested under a large tree and ate some of the food and drank some of the water.

To see all this happen made Kaia very angry. She gritted her teeth and stomped her foot. How could they be so unkind to their own children?

"Those horrible monsters… I wish…I just wish…"

"Kaia, no!" shouted Stefan shouted at her.

But it was too late.

"I wish they would just turn into two horrible looking toads!"

Immediately, Jinn sent up a shower of twinkling sparks which came together in midair and formed themselves into two shiny arrows which then shot off at high speed through the trees. Pleased with herself, Jinn held up her fingers and blew the tops, like the cowboys did in the old Wild West films after they had fired a shot.

Stefan could hardly keep himself from laughing out loud as he imagined the two parents turned into frogs. But that would have to wait until later because Hansel and Gretel were busy looking for the trail of breadcrumbs to lead them home.

"I'm sure it was here," Hansel was heard saying as he searched the ground.

"Maybe it was on the other side and you just got mixed up because you were tired," Gretel said.

They kept looking around in the forest, but they could not find the trail of breadcrumbs that Hansel had so careful left in the forest. Just as they got to the edge of the woods, a black bird swooped past them with a big piece of bread in its mouth. Both Hansel and Gretel froze and stared at each other.

"Oh no!" wailed Gretel, "The birds have eaten up all the bread! We are never going to get home now. We are lost forever!"

With that she buried her face in her hands and began to sob.

Hansel came over to her and put his arm around her shaking shoulders. "I'm sorry Gretel," he said sadly, "I thought it would work."

"What are we going to do now?" Gretel asked her brother.

"Well, we are not going to give up," he said… We're still going to try and find our way home. Come on, let's go!"

They started walking. On and on they walked through the woods until the sun was high up in the sky.

"I think we are lost, Hansel, and we'll never find our way back home." She sat down under an oak tree. "And I'm so hungry and thirsty. I must stop and rest." Gretel said.

Hansel tried to coax his sister to continue for just a little while longer. "Let's go through these bushes and see what's on the other side. Then we will rest, okay?"

Gretel followed her brother through the very thick patch of bushes. There was no path to follow and Gretel's clothes kept getting caught on the branches. She held on tightly to Hansel's hand as he helped her along.

As they followed the children, Stefan, Kaia and Jinn were finding it hard to stay out of sight and to not make any noise. They made sure to stay as far behind as possible.

As Hansel pulled Gretel through the last clump of bushes, they came to a sight that made them immediately stand still, gasping and with their eyes open wide.

Jinn, Kaia and Stefan finally caught up with them, but stayed low and out of sight off to the side of the clearing. But they also could not believe what they were seeing. They had read the story a million times and had imagined what the witch's house would look like, but never had they thought it would look like this.

There before them stood a huge cottage made entirely of sugary treats. There were candy canes and chocolate bars and sweets of every size, shape and color. The roof was made of red licorice twists and the window panes were made

47

of frosted sugar. Around the windows were fudge sticks and the door was one huge brownie. The walls were decorated with cakes, cherries and donuts and there were sweets mixed in between with all kinds of patterns.

The garden path leading up to the doorway was made of monster sized chocolate slabs and the cement holding them in place was the most golden caramel that any of them had ever seen. On either side of the doorway were two huge trees, but instead of having blossoms or fruit growing on them, these had sweets looking like every color of the rainbow. There were colorful pots that were scattered around the garden and each one contained a different sweet plant. One had toffees, the other had bubble gum, a third had red sweets that looked like cherries and yet

another was full of huge many colored popsicles that were so big they would take you a week to finish!

"Oh my, Hansel, I'm so hungry, I am going to eat it all!" Gretel shouted and before he could stop her, she started running towards the house.

"No Gretel," Hansel shouted after her, "It might be a trick and we don't know who lives here! Wait for me!"

He ran after her to try and stop her from taking anything off the house. But it was too late. Gretel had made it up the path and reached out and grabbed a handful of sweets off the tree by the door. Just as she stuffed a whole bunch in her mouth, the door of the house suddenly opened and a tall, thin woman came out.

"The Witch," Stefan whispered excitedly, "Finally!"

Chapter 7 – Don't Get Caught In a Web of Lies

Jinn placed a hand onto Stefan's shoulder to hold him back.

"What?" he asked, trying to shake off her hand? "Let's go and save her."

"No," Jinn replied, "Not yet. Let's just wait and see what happens first before we go racing in there. If we mess this up the Fairy Queen is going to be mad with me!"

Stefan and Kaia reluctantly crept back behind the bushes from where they peeked out at the sweet house through a tiny gap in the branches.

The witch had by this time come outside into the bright midday sunshine. They saw that she was tall and slim, with shiny straight silver hair that hung down her back like a shimmering sheet all the way to her waist. She had on the whitest dress any of them had ever seen. It had long billowing sleeves that glittered as the slight breeze blew them about. They reached all the way down to the grass.

She moved as if she was floating on air as she approached Hansel and Gretel. They heard her greet

them in a soft musical voice and when she smiled at the children, they saw how truly beautiful she was.

She was nothing like the witch they had read about in their books.

"Hello children," she said, "Don't eat these sweets out here. Why don't you come inside and have some cake? I have just baked a fresh batch of rainbow cupcakes. Don't you smell them? Do come inside, you look tired."

Stefan and Kaia looked at each other in surprise. Wow, she was nice! They had always been told about a cackling old witch with a hump back, dirty clothes and a wart on the end of her hook nose.

"See?" Jinn said smugly, "I told you guys she wasn't evil!"

Magical Sweets in Story Time

"Okay, you were so right," Kaia said, "Let's go get her out of here. What are we waiting for? Now is the time to do something!"

"No Kaia, we have to wait," Jinn said, "remember our job is to rescue the White Witch and also catch Brother Grimm… and we have not seen him yet."

So the three of them moved a little closer to the sweet house to be able to hear and see better. They settled down behind the bushes and lay in wait, taking turns to keep a sharp look out for Brother Grimm.

Meanwhile inside the house, the witch had settled the children at the table with milk and rainbow cupcakes which they gobbled down quickly. She was now busy preparing them a healthy meal for dinner and the wonderful smell was carried by the wind out into the woods where the children were hiding. Immediately, Stefan's stomach began to rumble!

A little while later they watched through the window as Hansel and Gretel sat down at the kitchen table and started to eat steaming hot bowls of stew and freshly baked bread. The witch had also made them some pudding for dessert which the kids polished off in seconds.

They had never had such a delicious meal before in their entire lives! And their stomachs had never been this full.

After dinner, the White Witch led Hansel and Gretel upstairs, tucked them into warm and cozy beds and planted a loving kiss on each of their foreheads. With full tummies and feeling more loved

than they had since their mom had died, Hansel and Gretel fell into a happy sleep.

Night had fallen and Stefan and Kaia were getting very impatient. They were relaxing against a tree while Jinn kept watch on the house. Suddenly, Jinn called out softly to Stefan and Kaia to join her. She put a finger to her lips, telling them to be quiet.

"Finally!" Stefan thought, "Some action!"

They tiptoed as quietly as they could across to where Jinn was standing as she watched Brother Grimm creep into the house.

"Come on," Jinn whispered, "Let's go closer and look through the cottage window to see

Magical Sweets in Story Time

what he is up to. But we must be quiet because we don't want Brother Grimm to know we are around.

They waited until the door closed behind Brother Grimm and then quickly they dashed across the yard and pressed themselves up against the side of the house. Stefan and Kaia had never been surrounded by so many sweets before and could not help breaking off some of the sweets and eating them.

Stefan looked up, his face covered in powdered sugar, and saw Jinn frowning at him. He swallowed quickly and touched Kaia too so she would stop eating.

"Stop eating and pay attention…, please?" Jinn hissed.

"Sorry," mumbled Kaia through a mouthful of brownie.

The three of them stood up on tip-toes and looked in the window.

What a sight greeted them! Brother Grimm had tied the White Witch to a chair and was carrying a wriggling Hansel under his arm. Gretel was by the door trembling, a look of total fear on her face.

They watched as Brother Grimm pushed Hansel roughly into a cage. Then he started circling the cage and chanting. It was a strange sound. They had never heard such words before. He was speaking a different language. As he moved around the cage the chants grew louder and louder.

Everyone was so busy watching Brother Grimm and Hansel that none of them saw that Gretel was no longer there. It was not until Kaia, out of the corner of her eye, saw something move. Quickly, she tugged on Jinn's arm.

They looked to see Gretel running across the grass and disappearing inside the woodshed. She came out a few minutes dragging a huge ax. But she was such a tiny girl and it was too heavy for her to carry.

"Should we help her?" Kaia asked.

But before Jinn could answer, Stefan said, "Oh no!"

Magical Sweets in Story Time

Merriweather Hope

Jinn and Kaia turned their attention back to what was happening inside the cottage. As Brother Grimm was chanting, the shape of a huge book appeared before him. It became clearer and clearer as he chanted. After a few seconds, the book thudded to the floor and a magical black and gold pen appeared and began writing in the book all by itself.

Stefan began trying to make out the words and saw that the pen was writing the story of Hansel and Gretel, but it wasn't writing the truth – it was writing the wrong story, a whole bunch of lies!

As the pen continued writing lies, Stefan, Kaia and Jinn watched as a tiny little black tornado started to form in the middle of the book. The wind from it got stronger and stronger and started to pull at the White Witch's clothes and hair.

"Oh no!" shouted Jinn, "She is being drawn into the book. This is how he has been trapping the magical creatures. We have to do something now!"

By the time they burst into the room, a huge hairy black spider web had sprouted out of the center of the tornado. Brother Grimm's web of lies was busy twisting itself all around the White Witch's ankles and was creeping up her legs.

"Statue, Statue of ice so cold, Freeze in place and release your hold," Jinn began to chant over and over again. It was a freezing spell that she knew the older genies could do but as she chanted another branch of the lie web started making its way over to her. She wiggled her fingers and set off an arrow of sharp purple darts in the direction of Brother Grimm. The web of lies rose up off the floor and tried to cover Brother Grimm from the freezing spell.

Jinn was so scared when she saw the web coming for her that she stumbled over some of the words and her spell went wrong. Instead of the darts flying directly at Brother Grimm and stopping him, they split into two groups. One group hit Brother Grimm all over his body but the other group was heading straight for the White Witch. She was still tied up and couldn't do anything but sit helplessly and watch as the darts flew towards her.

"No!" screamed Jinn, but it was too late. The purple darts hit the White Witch and knocked her out. She froze just like a statue and could not move. Jinn looked over at Brother Grimm and he too was frozen. He had stopped chanting and the magical pen had stopped writing.

"What now?" Stefan asked. He was so amazed by what he just saw that he felt as if the purple darts had hit him too.

Before Jinn could even reply the three of them watched as Brother Grimm somehow unfroze from the spell. He then snapped his fingers and disappeared along with the big book and the magical pen.

Jinn let out a loud groan and slapped a hand to her forehead. She was going to be in BIG trouble with the Fairy Queen for letting Brother Grimm get away!

Magical Sweets in Story Time

Chapter 8 – The Bad Guy Gets Away… Again

For a minute they all seemed frozen in time. Jinn was standing still, staring in surprise at what had just happened. At the moment she did not seem to have the power to do anything. It was up to Kaia to do something, anything to help.

She rushed over to the cage and quickly set Hansel free. Then turned around and shouted, "Stefan, don't just stand there, do something!"

Stefan looked at her and then over at the White Witch and Jinn. There was only one thing he could think of to do.

"I wish for the White Witch and Jinn to come back to being their real selves!" He shouted.

Immediately, the White Witch stopped being frozen from the genie's spell Jinn also came out of the trance she was in.

"Thanks Stefan, "Jinn said. "That was the weirdest feeling I ever had. Even though I knew I shouldn't, somehow I was becoming caught up in the web of lies that Brother Grimm was spinning. My head is so much clearer now."

"I'm so glad that you got free in time," said Stefan, smiling at her. He was glad she was back to her old self.

Just as everyone started talking together, Gretel came bursting through the door, dragging the ax behind her. She took one look at everyone's faces and then quickly fixed her eyes on Hansel.

"Who are all these people?" she asked, "What happened?"

Hansel told her everything that took place while she was outside. But one thing he could not tell her – who were Jinn, Kaia and Stefan and why they were there.

"I'm Jinn," said the genie, holding out her hand to Gretel, "and this is Kaia and Stefan." She told Hansel and Gretel how they came to be there and that they were only there to help and not to hurt them.

"So you see, "Jinn finished, "We really needed to catch Brother Grimm to stop him from being able to do this to anyone else. He has gotten away with this for way too long.

"Right then," said Hansel feeling very brave,

Magical Sweets in Story Time

"Let's go and look for him. There are six of us now and I am sure we can catch him."

"I couldn't agree more," said Stefan, "We can't let him keep getting away after everything he has done. Let's go and find him now. He can't be too far away."

"I don't know," said Gretel, who was still feeling a little bit scared. "But we don't even know where to start looking?"

"That's right," agreed Kaia, "he just disappeared like that. He could be anywhere. How would we know where to go without any clues?"

At that point, the White Witch stood up and spoke. She turned to Jinn, Stefan and Kaia and said in her musical voice, "Firstly, thank you for saving me. If you hadn't come in when you did I don't know what would have happened to me or where I would have ended up."

Jinn and the children felt happy they were able to help free her. They all knew they had kept her from being trapped in Grimm's story book and being forever called a bad person.

"Now children, Kaia is right," she continued, "We have no idea where to go to find Brother Grimm and without some sort of a clue it is just far too dangerous. I do not want any harm to come to any of you, especially after what you have just been through."

"Yes, "Jinn chimed in, "Although we didn't catch Brother Grimm, we rescued you, so we saved a bit of magic. I'm sure when we tell this to the Fairy Queen she will not be so angry with me."

As Jinn said this she crossed her fingers hard behind her back and said a silent prayer that she really was not going to be in too much trouble with the Fairy Queen again!

Chapter 9 – Everyone Gets to Go Home With a Full Tummy

"Before we go anywhere, let's celebrate!" said the White Witch, "Before Brother Grimm came bursting in here I had just baked some delicious magical treats."

They all sat down around her table and began to eat. Kaia and Stefan were so hungry, they gobbled up the cakes greedily. It felt like days since they had last eaten and with all the excitement and adventure they were starving! The White Witch served the cakes with a glittering bubbling blue juice that seemed to have diamonds inside. It was better than anything either of them had ever tasted before.

"Wow!" whispered Stefan, "This stuff is amazing!"

"I know," Kaia agreed, "I wish we could take some back home with us."

After they had helped the White Witch to clear up the dishes and clean up her kitchen, they all set off to take Hansel and Gretel back home. Luckily the White Witch knew the woods really

Merriweather Hope

well and led them straight to the tiny little cottage in no time at all.

As they came into the clearing, Stefan suddenly grabbed Kaia by the arm and said, "Kaia, you wished for Hansel and Gretel's parents to be turned into toads. They are going to find the house empty when they go inside."

"Oh my gosh, I forgot about that," Kaia replied, "I had better wish for them to be human again, especially since one of our rules was not to hurt anyone."

She turned to Jinn who was standing to the left of her and said, "Jinn, I wish for Hansel and Gretel's parents not to be frogs anymore."

She looked over at Jinn then and added, happily, "I also wish for them to be nicer to Hansel and Gretel and never to treat them badly again."

With that, Jinn shot a rainbow of colorful sparks up into the air and over the clearing towards the cottage. The end of the rainbow disappeared through one of the windows and the next minute the whole house seemed to glow brightly like the sun.

Magical Sweets in Story Time

Hansel and Gretel looked over at Jinn in fright.

"Don't worry," she told them, "It's safe to go home now."

They all gave Hansel and Gretel each a goodbye hug and as the children crossed the clearing hand in hand, they turned and waved to Stefan, Kaia, Jinn and the White Witch.

That's when Stefan suddenly had a brilliant idea. He turned to Kaia and said, "All of this happened because they didn't have enough food to eat, right?"

"Yeah," replied Kaia, "It's so sad."

"Don't worry," Stefan said, "I have a plan!"

Kaia looked at him carefully. She hoped it would not be another one that would get them into trouble. He was good at doing that.

Stefan turned to Jinn and with a huge grin spreading across his face he said, "Jinn, I wish that Hansel and Gretel's family will never go hungry again. I want you to make sure they will always have enough to eat."

Jinn looked at him with pride. How kind he was making wishes to help others instead of just for himself! As she grinned back at him about a hundred tiny little silver tornados shot out of all of Jinn's fingers and made their way over to the cottage.

"What are you doing, Jinn?" the White Witch asked.

"Oh I'm just filling up Hansel and Gretel's house with an endless amount of food. As soon as one thing is finished, another one will appear in its place. It's quite fancy magic," she said proudly.

Then she winked at Stefan and said, "I gave them a never-ending supply of Magical Charms cereal too. Perhaps it will bring them some luck."

As they all stood watching Hansel and Gretel go into the house and close the door with a final wave, Kaia let out a big yawn.

"You two must be tired," the White Witch said.

Magical Sweets in Story Time

Now that all the excitement was over, Stefan was feeling tired. "Yeah," he said, "It's been a busy few days."

"Let's go home," Kaia said. "We are going to have a lot of explaining to do to our parents."

At that Jinn just gave them both a mysterious smile and wiggled her eyebrows at Stefan. "You know what to do," she said.

Stefan covered a yawn, too tired to even guess what Jinn was up to now. He only said, "I wish we could all be back in my bedroom."

And the next minute they were all traveling at top speed back through the time travel tunnel once again.

Chapter 10 – It's Never Too Late for Magical Adventures

They landed with a thud in a heap on the floor in Stefan's small bedroom. As they were picking themselves up and fixing their clothes, Stefan heard the front door open.

Stefan and Kaia looked at each other, prepared for the trouble they were going to be in for being missing for days. They still found it hard to believe that their parents had accepted the whole "saving magic" bit so easily!

"Stefan, Kaia," they heard Stefan's dad shout.

"Time to face Mom and Dad," Kaia said, "Come on Stefan, let's get it over with."

The kids walked to the top of the stair case and looked down at Stefan's dad.

"We're all done for the evening," he told them, "You are welcome to stay here for a little while Kaia, but not too late since it's a school night."

Stefan and Kaia looked at each other. What was going on? Did their parents not know that they had been away for a few days? They had no idea

Magical Sweets in Story Time

what was going on, but they were glad nobody was upset with them. Kaia just said thanks to Stefan's dad and then they went back inside.

As they opened the door, they saw Jinn hovering in mid-air over Stefan's desk where her lamp still lay. She was doubled over with laughter. The sound was beautiful, just like the tinkling of bells.

"Jinn!" Stefan said as sternly as he could. He had just found out that she had something to do with their parents' behavior. "Tell me right now, what did you do to our parents?

"Well," she said, clearly enjoying herself, "When we time travel into Story Time, time in the world of humans stands still. That means your parents did not know you were gone much less to miss you."

As she grinned at them, both Stefan and Kaia just stood there staring at her. How come they never knew that? Oh, this was very good news. Not having to tell where they had been meant they did not have to tell any lies. They could just pick up where they had left off before they had set off on their adventure.

Merriweather Hope

As this sunk in, both Kaia and Stefan laughed out loud. They had been on such an amazing adventure. They could still hardly believe it had really happened. All four of them began chatting about it, remembering different bits and pieces. Their adventure was better than anything Stefan's imagination could have dreamed up.

They knew they would be seeing a lot more of Jinn and had plenty more new and exciting adventures ahead of them because they still had to capture Brother Grimm and save magic.

Stefan's began to think of all the exciting things that could happen next time. Perhaps in the next adventure he would get to zoom off into space to fight aliens. Who knew what lay ahead?

While Stefan was busy daydreaming, the White Witch came up to him and placed her hand on his shoulder and cleared her throat. She smiled down at him gently and said, "Stefan, It's time for us to go now, but before I do, I have something for you and Kaia to thank you for setting me free."

She pulled out two oval shaped objects and held them out in the palm of her hand. They were wrapped in shiny red paper with golden swirls

Magical Sweets in Story Time

that glittered and glowed. She handed one to Stefan and the other to Kaia.

"These are special magical sweets," she told them, "Keep them for a time when you really need my help and I will come."

"Wow!" Kaia said, "Thank you."

"Thank you," Stefan said.

"Right," Jinn said, "Time to go. See you guys sooner than you think." And she was smiling mischievously.

The White Witch and Jinn joined hands facing one another and began to turn in circles together. Seconds later they were moving so fast they were nothing but a blur. They then shot up, bounced off the ceiling, disappeared down the spout of the magic lamp and were gone.

Epilogue – Time is Running Out for Magic…

The old lamp clattered to the stone floor outside a huge beautifully decorated iron door.

"Ophelia, go and see what made that awful noise," came a voice from inside.

"Yes, Your Majesty," Ophelia replied.

Slowly the doors to the throne room opened and Ophelia gasped. "Your Majesty, come quickly," she shouted.

"What is it?" asked the Fairy Queen, joining her at the door. As she saw what Ophelia was looking at she also gasped.

"My sister!" she exclaimed joyfully rushing forward to hug the White Witch who was standing next to Jinn.

"Jinn, you have returned my sister to me so she can claim her rightful place beside me in the magical realm. Thank you. I am so proud of you," she said with great joy.

Magical Sweets in Story Time

"It's my pleasure, Your Majesty," Jinn said with a polite curtsy, very pleased with the Fairy Queen's praise.

"Do come inside," the Fairy Queen said. "I want to hear all the details of how Brother Grimm came to his end."

"Oh dear," thought Jinn, fear gripping her. "Here goes."

"Well, um, you see Your Majesty, um well, that's actually a funny story," Jinn stammered and tried to laugh.

The Fairy Queen immediately raised an eyebrow and said in a harsh voice, "Explain yourself right now!"

"Well, see, um, we didn't catch him exactly," Jinn said while looking at the floor.

"What?" shrieked the Fairy Queen, "You mean you let him get away?"

"Well, um…no…" Jinn stuttered.

"Well, get on with it then, where is he?" she shouted, growing angrier by the minute.

"Um, well, see, I'm not really sure where he is. He just kind of disappeared into the air," Jinn mumbled quietly while twisting her hands together nervously.

The Fairy Queen's yelling was deafening and Jinn had to try hard not to cover her ears. "I cannot believe that you let him get away! Do you know how serious is the situation?"

But before the Fairy Queen could say anymore, Jinn jumped in and said, "I'm so sorry, Your Majesty, but there was a lot going on and…"

"Don't you dare interrupt me when I'm talking to you!" The Queen roared.

Jinn hung her head. She hated being in trouble, all she wanted was to please the Fairy Queen.

The Queen quieted down a bit before saying, "You know what he has been doing and you knew how important it was to catch him. Now once again you are standing here telling me you did not finish the job I sent you to do. "Her voice got softer and a little kinder. "It's not that I want to be angry with you. But time is running out, Jinn. The last dragon egg is about to hatch and you know what that means…."

To Be Continued...

Merriweather Hope

If you enjoyed this book please share the love and leave a review on Amazon – it really helps out new authors like me!

Good news is always welcome.

Thanks a ton and I'll see you in the next adventure!

Merriweather Hope

Magical Sweets in Story Time

Don't miss book three in the "Fairy Tales & Magical Adventures" series!

In *"Dragons at Dessert Time,"* Jinn, Stefan, and Kaia are joined by two new companions in their quest to save magic!

Stefan's best friend Adam has been feeling left out because Stefan's been spending all his time with Kaia (he thinks Kaia is Stefan's girlfriend!) so Stefan and Kaia decide to tell him about all the secret adventures they've been having.

Little do they know, but Adam has a magical item of his own – a little dragon Magical Charm – and when Jinn shows up and turns it into a REAL dragon named Fire, the friends very quickly find themselves on another adventure.

Merriweather Hope

Now time is running out, and Stefan, Kaia, Jinn, Adam, and Fire have to travel through story time in search of the dragon's lair to try and reunite the last surviving dragons before they all disappear forever!

"Jinn began to chant her spell…

"Magical universe hear my call,

Transport us through the vortex wall,

Get us safely from here to there,

To rescue the Princess from Brother Grimm's lair"

As she finished speaking, she raised her right hand and sent up a bright red ray of light out of her fingers. It formed a red cloud and when Jinn clicked her fingers it started to rain.

Hundreds of drops of golden liquid began to fall on them. Kaia watched as the drops hit her arm and the places where it touched her, began to disappear. It was almost as if someone was using a giant eraser to rub her out. She looked around and saw that everyone else seemed to also be disappearing.

The next minute, a huge flash of golden lightning shot out of the clouds. It hit the floor just in front of where they were standing. This opened up a huge swirling hole in the ground. It was like when you pulled the plug out the bath and all the water swirled around as it ran down the drain. Only this was more like a volcano because the colors were red and gold like hot lava.

"Get ready. When I say so, jump into the vortex," Jinn told them.

"Jump!" shouted Jinn a few moments later....

Merriweather Hope

The last thing Kaia saw as they all jumped into the vortex was Stefan's huge grin. "Never a dull moment when Jinn's around," she thought.

Get your copy of "Dragons at Dessert Time" to see what happens next...

http://www.amazon.com/dp/B00OYLB1AE

Made in the USA
Charleston, SC
11 December 2014